The story of Jacob is retold simply and
delightfully illustrated for young readers.

Note to parents and teachers
*The Biblical account of the patriarch Jacob can be found in
Genesis, chapters 27 to 36. Jacob is shown as a schemer and
trickster who, in turn, is tricked himself. But his story illustrates
the idea that God's purposes may be accomplished through
unlikely vessels. For it is Jacob who is given the name 'Israel',
inherits God's promises to Abraham and Isaac, and becomes the
direct ancestor of the twelve tribes of Israel.*

British Library Cataloguing in Publication Data
Hately, David
    Jacob.
    1. Bible. O.T. Genesis. Jacob — Stories for children
I. Title   II. Breeze, Lynn
III. [Bible. O.T. Genesis. *English. Selections. 1988*]   IV. Series
222'.110924
    ISBN 0-7214-1111-8

First edition

Published by Ladybird Books Ltd Loughborough Leicestershire UK
Ladybird Books Inc Auburn Maine 04210 USA

© LADYBIRD BOOKS LTD MCMLXXXVIII

Printed in England

Jacob

written by David Hately
illustrated by Lynn Breeze

Ladybird Books

Isaac and his wife Rebecca had been married for many years, but they had no children. Then, to their great joy, they learned that Rebecca was going to have twins.

When the time came, she gave birth to two boys. One they named Esau; the other, Jacob.

Esau grew up to be a hunter. He liked nothing better than being outdoors all day long.

Jacob became a skilled herdsman. He was quieter than his brother and preferred to stay at home.

Esau was older than Jacob by a minute or so. This meant that one day he would be the head of the family and inherit everything that belonged to his father. It was his birthright.

One evening he arrived home tired and hungry, and found Jacob busy making some spicy soup. It smelled so good that he called out, 'I'd give anything for a share of your soup!'

'All right!' answered Jacob slyly. 'I'll let you have some if you'll give me your birthright!'

'Here's me starving to death,' laughed Esau, 'and you talk about birthrights! Just give me a bowl of soup!'

'Only if you promise,' insisted Jacob.

Now the smell of the soup was so delicious that Esau would have promised anything. 'All right, all right!' he said, still laughing. 'I agree!'

So Jacob gave his brother some soup and a hunk of bread. But when he was alone, he smiled his crafty smile and thought how clever he'd been.

As Isaac got older, he began to lose his eyesight. One day he sent for Esau, who was his favourite son. 'It's time I gave you my blessing,' he said. 'It will make you the head of our family, and when I die you will inherit everything.'

Before giving the blessing, however, Isaac asked Esau to catch some wild game and cook it for him as a special treat.

But Rebecca was listening. She had a plan to cheat Esau of his birthright. For Jacob was her favourite, and she wanted him to get the blessing.

'Bring me two kid goats,' Rebecca said to Jacob. 'I know how to cook them so that they'll taste like wild game. Then, if you take the dish to your father, he'll think you're Esau, and he'll give *you* the blessing! You will inherit everything.'

'What if my father touches me?'
asked Jacob. 'My skin is as smooth
as silk, but Esau's is rough and hairy.'

'I know what I'm doing,' replied
Rebecca. 'Just bring me the two
kids.'

When Rebecca had cooked the two young goats she covered Jacob's arms and neck with the hairy goatskins. Then Jacob carried the dish in to his father, and pretended to be Esau.

When he spoke, he tried to make his voice sound deep, like Esau's. But Isaac was suspicious. He stretched out his hand to touch Jacob's smooth skin, and felt the rough hair of the goatskins.

'The voice is like Jacob's,' he said to himself, 'but there's no mistaking Esau's skin!'

Then Isaac kissed his son, and gave Jacob the blessing meant for Esau.

When Esau returned from hunting, the trick was discovered. Isaac trembled with anger, and Esau was in despair. 'Have you no blessing for me?' he cried to his father.

But Isaac answered, 'It's too late. I have already made Jacob your master.'

Esau burst into tears, crying as though his heart would break. He hated Jacob for his treachery, and made up his mind to kill him as soon as their father was dead.

Rebecca knew what Esau was planning. She persuaded Jacob to seek safety with her brother, whose name was Laban. He lived far away in a place called Haran.

So Jacob fled. He didn't know if he would ever see his home again. His cheating had done him no good after all.

One night, on the way to Haran, he dreamed a vivid dream. It seemed that a stairway stretched from earth to heaven. Angels – the messengers of God – passed up and down it to carry out God's commands.

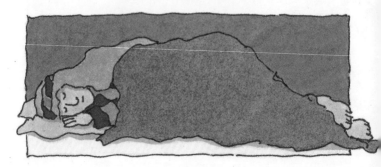

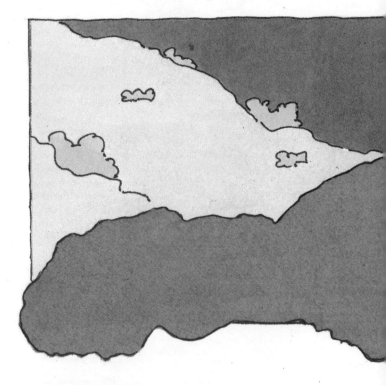

In his dream, Jacob heard God speaking to him.

I will give you and your descendants the ground on which you are lying, the voice said. **Your children's children will outnumber the specks of dust on the ground. I am**

always with you, and I will keep you safe wherever you go.

When Jacob woke up, he began to understand that God wanted him for some special purpose. 'Even though I'm a cheat and a liar,' he said to himself, 'God is still with me.'

Jacob continued his journey and at
last reached the land of Haran. He
stopped by a well, where some sheep
were being watered, and asked a
shepherd if he knew a man called
Laban.

'Yes!' came the reply. 'That's his daughter over there. She's a shepherdess. Her name is Rachel.'

And as soon as Jacob saw the girl, he knew that he wanted her to be his wife.

Jacob was made welcome by Laban and his family. He worked hard tending the flocks, but refused to take any wages.

'This isn't fair!' said Laban. 'I don't expect you to work for nothing! What should I pay you?'

'I'll work for nothing for seven years,' answered Jacob, 'if you'll then let me marry Rachel.'

Laban looked thoughtful, but at last he agreed to the bargain.

Jacob loved Rachel so much that the seven years flew by.

At last, it was time for the marriage feast. As Jacob went to embrace his wife, the girl removed the veil which hid her face, and Jacob saw that he had been cheated! His bride was not Rachel – it was her older sister, Leah!

'Why have you done this to me?' he asked angrily.

'Because in our country,' Laban answered, 'we never allow the younger daughter to marry before the older.'

So Jacob found out what it was like to be cruelly tricked.

At that time, the law said that a man could marry two sisters. So, after another seven years' hard work, Jacob married Rachel.

The years passed and Jacob grew rich, for he used his skill with animals to build up fine, sturdy flocks. But he was not really happy in Haran. He wanted to go back to his homeland in Canaan.

Above all, he wanted to make peace with his brother Esau.

So Jacob and his family set off for Canaan. He had learned that Esau was living in the land of Edom, and when he reached its borders he stopped.

He decided to send messengers on ahead to greet his brother. But the messengers returned to tell him that Esau was riding towards them with a force of four hundred men.

Jacob was afraid. He was sure that Esau wanted revenge.

Then Jacob remembered God's promise. 'You said that you would keep me safe and make me prosper,' he prayed. 'Keep your promise!'

All night, it seemed to Jacob that he struggled with God in a wrestling match. His hip bone was pulled out of joint, but still he fought on. And at last God gave Jacob the blessing he wanted.

He also gave him a new name. He called him Israel, which means 'the one who fought with God'.

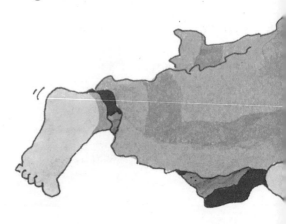

When Jacob left the place where he had wrestled with God, he was limping because of his injured hip. He said, 'It means death for a man to look on God, but I have seen him face to face and lived to tell the tale.'

After his struggle with God, Jacob was a changed man. With his new name he began a new life. He realised that his fortune came through the power of God's blessing, not through his own cleverness.

When it was time to meet his brother, Jacob decided that he would try to sweeten Esau's anger.

He chose about five hundred of the best animals from his flocks and divided them into groups. He put each group into the care of a servant, and one by one the servants drove their animals towards Esau. They told Esau that Jacob had sent them as a gift.

Jacob and his brother at last came face to face, and Esau cried out, 'What on earth is going on? Why are you sending me all these animals?'

'Because I want you to forgive me for stealing your birthright,' Jacob answered.

And, to Jacob's amazement, Esau burst out laughing!

Esau took his brother Jacob in his arms and hugged him. Soon his laughter changed to tears of joy at seeing his brother again.

'I don't want your animals!' he said to Jacob. 'I don't want anything from you. I have plenty of everything.' So the brothers became firm friends, and went back together to their father.

Isaac, who was now very old, was full of pride and joy at having his sons with him once more.

But Esau decided that the land of Canaan was not for him. It could not support his own flocks as well as those belonging to Jacob, so he took his family and settled in a land nearby.

But Jacob lived on at home with his wives and children. He knew that his people would grow into a great nation, because God had promised it and he trusted God.

Jacob had been a trickster all his life, until he'd seen God face to face. Now, Jacob understood God's power.